The Queen's Caprice

Also By Jean Echenoz

The Queen's Caprice

Stories

Jean Echenoz

Translated by Linda Coverdale

THE NEW PRESS

NEW YORK
LONDON

The New Press gratefully acknowledges the Florence Gould
Foundation for supporting the publication of this book.

Originally published in France as *Caprice de la
reine*, Les Éditions de Minuit, Paris, 2014
Published in the United States by The New Press, New York, 2015
Distributed by Perseus Distribution

LIBRARY OF CONGRESS CATALOGING-IN-PUBLICATION DATA

Echenoz, Jean.
[Short stories. Selections. English]
The queen's caprice : stories / Jean Echenoz ; translated by Linda Coverdale.
pages cm
Includes bibliographical references.
ISBN 978-1-62097-065-2 (hardcover : alk. paper)—
ISBN 978-1-62097-072-0 (e-book)
1. Echenoz, Jean—Translations into English. 2. Short stories,
French. 3. French fiction—21st century. I. Coverdale,
Linda. II. Echenoz, Jean. Caprice de la reine. English III. Title.
PQ2665.C5A2 2015
843'.914—dc23   2014047909

The New Press publishes books that promote and enrich public
discussion and understanding of the issues vital to our democracy and to
a more equitable world. These books are made possible by the enthusiasm
of our readers; the support of a committed group of donors, large and
small; the collaboration of our many partners in the independent media
and the not-for-profit sector; booksellers, who often hand-sell New Press
books; librarians; and above all by our authors.

www.thenewpress.com

Composition by dix!
This book was set in Stempel Garamond

Printed in the United States of America

2   4   6   8   10   9   7   5   3   1

CONTENTS

TRANSLATOR'S NOTE

For the publication in English of his *Caprice de la reine,* Jean Echenoz has made a few minor changes in the texts. These seven *récits* are his favorite occasional pieces, written on subjects that inspired the author to observe, improvise, invent—for although these stories sometimes spring from historical incident, they are in the end what Echenoz wished to create: "little literary objects."

This tension between story and history depends in part on the ability of the reader to catch allusions and follow undercurrents of meaning that are reasonably clear to French readers but may pass completely unnoticed in English. I have therefore provided endnotes for some of these references and for a few other points of interest as well.

—Linda Coverdale

The Queen's Caprice

NELSON

WINTER 1802, MANOR HOUSE in the English countryside, Admiral Nelson is coming to dinner. The other
guests hurry over as soon as he appears in the drawing
room among the candelabra, wall hangings, copper- and
brassware, ancestral portraits, floral paintings, flow-
ers. Although still battle-worn from the engagement at
Copenhagen,[1] he is admired; he does look tired, they
reflect, but my he's handsome think the ladies. Tired, of
course, and rightly so, after all he's been through.

Already—so awkward for a sailor—there'd been
that affliction he had experienced as a thirteen-year-old
seaman upon first joining a warship, the third-rate
HMS *Raisonnable.* He had thought it would pass but

no, he had never ceased to suffer terribly, day after day, throughout his thirty years at sea, from seasickness.

So they fuss over him, this man in an armchair near the large window overlooking some ingeniously informal gardens bordered by underbrush and backed by a wall of trees. Brandishing a tray of quivering glasses, a footman leans toward Nelson, who plucks one of them with a languid hand. Nelson is a small, thin man, affable, youthful in appearance, very handsome indeed but perhaps a trifle pale. And though he smiles like an actor playing Admiral Nelson, he seems quite fragile, friable, on the verge of fracturing into pieces.

A slender form wearing white stockings, steel-buckled shoes, white waistcoat and knee-breeches under a blue frock coat, of which the left pocket bulges with what seems like a handful of shillings and the left breast glitters with the Order of the Bath. Nelson's eyes sparkle as well but each with a different luster, the right one less brightly than the other. And if his hand hesitates in picking up his glass, the problem is that having contracted malaria in the Indies about twenty-five years earlier, while serving on the frigate HMS *Seahorse,* he has been plagued ever since by recurrent fevers, headaches, polyneuritis, and the attendant tremors.

Since the conversation in the drawing room concerns the Treaty of Amiens, the admiral's attention is drawn to a delicate point regarding the evacuation of the island of Elba; he is handed a newspaper that addresses the matter. Nelson places the page to his left, at an angle, and seems able to read it only in this manner, sideways—for another problem is that during the bombardment of Calvi in Corsica, while he was in command of the sixty-four-gun HMS *Agamemnon,* the impact of a round shot showered his face with stone shards that cost him the vision in his right eye.[2]

Everyone sits down to dinner and even though small portions have been precut for the admiral, he displays deft skill in plying his knife and fork with his one hand—for yet another problem is that while his flagship HMS *Theseus* lay off Santa Cruz de Tenerife, where Nelson attempted to seize the port city so as to relieve enemy ships of their gold bullion, he was hit by a musket ball that, fracturing his humerus in several places, deprived him of the use of his promptly amputated right arm.

Left left-handed, the admiral had therefore to re-learn how to write and how to eat with utensils at the table—although he does resort daily to opium to relieve the pain in his phantom limb—and he acquits himself handsomely: the dinner proceeds without a hitch. Upon observing, however, that twilight is coming on, that candlesticks will soon be carried in, Nelson now rises abruptly between two courses, requests somewhat stiffly that the company please excuse him for a few minutes, and withdraws. He leaves the dining room, passes through antechambers and sitting rooms, then goes outside to the garden while the guests look at one another and frown.

Thus one-eyed, one-armed, and feverish, the admiral finds himself among the flower beds and clumps of shrubs before going off on his own toward the woods, incidentally passing a garden shed where he borrows a full watering can. He advances into the fading daylight; he loves the contemplation of countryside, woods, and forests. He could almost live there but, rather anxious to return to sea, he prefers to visit other people's homes to perform the following operation.

At the edge of the wood, Nelson paces off the

distance to the first trees: measuring, he selects various spots about twenty yards apart and marks each of them with a pebble. Kneeling at the first place, he begins digging a hole two to three inches deep—not so easy with only one hand, but the admiral is handy with his. The job done, he feels around in his pocket to pull out not the imagined handful of shillings but a dozen acorns, placing one at the bottom of this hole he then fills in again, carefully tamping down the earth he next waters just enough, he thinks (a touch too much, actually), after which Nelson repeats this operation as many times as his supply of acorns allows.

For he takes the very long view of things: he is retimbering and never passes up an opportunity, when away from the open sea on dry land, to sow the latter to ensure on the former, for future generations, adequate naval traffic. He has set his heart on planting trees whose trunks will serve to build the future royal fleet. From these acorns he buries will spring the masts, hulls, decks and 'tweendecks of every manner of vessel destined for commerce or the transportation of men—but warships of all kinds above all: ships of the line, corvettes, armored vessels, frigates, and destroyers that will sail the world's oceans long after he is gone, for the greater glory of the empire.

Yet the stout oaks of Suffolk serve not only to build ships: kegs and casks are also made from them—barrels that are carried aboard ships, moreover, and which can be of goodly service. In that vein, at Trafalgar, after the French sailor Guillemard[3] draws a bead on Nelson pacing the deck of the HMS *Victory,* and once the musket ball enters the admiral's body through the left shoulder, fracturing the acromion plus the second and third ribs, traversing the lung and slicing through a branch of the pulmonary artery before shattering his spine, everyone will wonder what to do with his corpse. Then they will recall that the admiral had desired, instead of being tossed overboard as dead sailors usually are, to be buried at home. To preserve Nelson until his return to England, he will therefore be immersed in a barrel of brandy, which will be sealed, strapped to the ship's mainmast, and placed under close armed guard.

The Queen's Caprice

To the right of the hand writing this lies first a terrace of faux pebble-stone tiles, with a balustrade topped by an aluminum handrail and formed by a series of Plexiglas panels through which we see the lower part of the panorama. This terrace overlooks a vast, triangular, and gently sloping lawn extending at its lower end into a more abrupt declivity, almost a bluff, bordered by a grove of evergreen oaks below which, when the wind is favorable, an invisible torrent sends muted news of its progress. So the bluff leads into a trough one might qualify as a trench, a canyon, or, more simply, a ravine. Let's go with ravine.

On the far side of this ravine, directly opposite, through the intertwined branches of evergreen oaks, can be seen a distant path that forms the horizontal baseline of a field sloped in symmetry with the lawn and, at its high end, bounded by hedgerows enclosing some pasture occupied by what will have to be called cows. These, aside from grazing, seem to have no other preoccupation in life than adjusting their position according to that of the sun, depending on whether or not they feel the need for some shade. This group, which is perhaps a herd and numbers no more than twenty individuals, is due south. Fine. Let us now circulate from the south toward the east then the north and so on counterclockwise, taking a complete tour of the horizon until we later arrive back at the herd and see if these cows have, in the meantime, moved.

On their left is a farm, to which we may assume these animals belong, along with buildings we can only partially see: first off, a large expanse of wall solidly capped with a slate roof, apparently part of some residential buildings, properly speaking; next, adjoining those and roofed with what should perhaps be identified as Everite tiles, is the visible part of another construction that is probably the annex, or one of the annexes of this operation. These structures, of which one can see only bits and pieces, are in fact barely visible amid the vegetation, and to the latter we shall return. We'll have to return to it although we could perhaps have—should perhaps have—begun with the vegetation, we don't know.

We don't know insofar as it is difficult in a description or a narrative, as Joseph Conrad has someone observe in his novella *A Smile of Fortune,* to set everything down in due order. It's just that one cannot say or describe everything all at the same time, can one. Some kind of order must be established, priorities set up, which can't help but risk muddling the subject, so we'll have to concentrate later on the vegetation, on nature, a framework no less important than the cultural objects—equipment, buildings—we are attempting at the outset to record.

After this almost indiscernible farm to the south, then a swath of forest we will accordingly try to describe more clearly further along, one should take note on the east-northeast axis of another farm not nearly so obscured as the first one, but also farther away. Although this time it's more like a cluster of farms, five or six, with walls and roofs of colors (dusty pink, spanking-new white, faded black, beige, and bright yellow) that vary and materials (slate or tile, stone, corrugated iron, pebble-dash, unidentified metal) just as diverse. Given how far away we are, say one or two miles from this little group of structures, we feel some hesitation: should one simply consider it a good-size farm, even a very good-size one, or may one venture to call it a hamlet? A dot on the landscape? Let's say a hamlet. Adjoining this hamlet, moreover, are a few of its classic attributes: a small road, a path, a bridge doubtless busy spanning the river that, rushing southward, has carved out the ravine. We can recognize them rather well, these attributes, for the intervening vegetation is somewhat sparse.

Perhaps now would be a good time to consider the importance of the vegetal realm in the matter at hand, which, since we're attempting to describe a particular setting in the Mayenne countryside,[1] is after all the very least we can do. So, vegetation. We already see in the complete southeastern arc how all these inhabited objects can be separated by heaps of trees almost exaggeratedly French in their exhaustively thorough sampling: oak, ash, beech, elm, lime, and the occasional species of more than one syllable, such as poplar. From the first farm to the hamlet, their density is absolute; their vertical compactness saturates the entire corresponding area on the other side of the ravine, leaving no room to breathe. But stepping back a little, which the morphology of the site will allow us to do as we head north, we will then be able to count on some open space: the varied horizontality of fields, meadows, fallow land, and other flat or undulating surfaces.

Onward, onward let us go toward the septentrion.[2] Whereas we earlier found ourselves, facing this ravine between us and the referential herd of cows, looking out as if on a promontory bung up against the opposite side of the ravine, now we must at first turn toward the north, looking up in a worm's-eye view. And to do this we must get going. Indeed, although from the terrace we were able to serenely observe the entire south and a good bit of the east from a sitting position, we must now get up to go take a look at the other cardinal axes.

We have to walk, to go around the house extended by this terrace and constructed on the flank of the promontory: the best thing to do would be to climb toward the hedgerow planted uphill from the building. The hedgerow, a line composed almost entirely of wild cherry trees, divides this private area from the countryside beyond. Standing at this border, we'll be able to observe the northern expanse extending, we won't say right to our feet but almost. That's why the vegetation, from this vantage point, seems less dense, for not only is it more scattered, but we are within a vastly larger field of vision, where objects are farther away and the plant life at that distance becomes less haughty, more humble, less arrogant and lofty. Plains, small valleys, thickets, hillocks, gentle rises. Perspective has edged out close encounters to the point of offering at the horizon of this suite of scenery the relief of a distant plateau: nothing less than the highest point, at barely 1,365 feet above sea level, of the entire Armorican massif. Aside from that, closer to us, floating above the décor and three-quarters concealed by an effervescence of vegetation, is a vaguely eighteenth-century castle: fragments of pinnacles, chimneys, and turrets. And that seems to be all.

It appears to be all because the entire west has neither rhyme nor reason. Once past that vast perspective to the north, one finds oneself back nose-to-nose with the here and now, with little things within arm's reach: woodpiles, tools, the black stain of some recently burned weeds, garden furniture. To the northwest lies the drivable road that, linked back to the local road and thus to the highway, allows access to the house. At the end of the circuit, a gentle wooded slope will soon rejoin the ravine. Let's finish our tour of this house, let's rejoin to the south the lawn, the terrace, the armchair, and the hand that, returning to its place, is finishing writing this. The cows don't appear to have moved much unless, after performing a frenetic ballet behind our backs, they have noticed our return and demurely resumed their original positions.

And at our feet, uncoiled on the terrace lies an orange garden hose, like a snake left for dead, and alongside which an abundant population of ants bustles in both directions, each ant staying mostly to the right as on a normal road. This traffic is quite dense and must link the ants' dormitories near their construction site to their various workshops, grain silos, mushroom farms, egg-laying laboratories, and aphid stables. Stopping briefly when they meet, the female workers execute some rapid frontal contact, just to exchange a surreptitious kiss or remind themselves of the password for the day, unless it's to have a quiet little laugh over the latest caprice of the queen.

In Babylon

In the center of a fertile plain, Babylon is a square city protected by considerable ramparts pierced by bronze gates and overlooking vast moats. Herodotus arrives there and, duly impressed, attempts to estimate the dimensions of these walls: evaluations in stades, cubits, and feet, which one is tempted at first to convert to metric but why bother. For it is not inconceivable that, carried away by his enthusiasm or fatigued by his voyage, Herodotus is exaggerating. Anyway, all authors exaggerate; they're all bent on contradicting one another. So let's say, to be brief, that the surface area of Babylon would be seven times that of modern Paris.

Once on site, Herodotus collects information. He would like to know in particular how the inhabitants went about constructing such a monumental city. First off, they explain to him, they dug ditches and then shaped and baked the earth into bricks. And that's how they began, by building the walls of Babylon: layers of bricks cemented with bitumen and separated at every thirtieth course by lattices of woven reeds. The reeds aren't a problem, they can be found just about everywhere; as for the bitumen, no need to look far for that: eight days' journey on foot from the city, the Is, a small affluent of the Euphrates, spits out gobs of it at its source.

As much an explorer as he is a historian, Herodotus also assures us that the city's ramparts are so wide that a four-horse chariot may pass along the top. There again we're not much enlightened, however, for Ctesias of Cnidus—physician to the king of Persia, whose court spends several months a year in Babylon—claims for his part that two chariots can pass each other there without any difficulty. Strabo will say the same thing, but Diodorus of Sicily cites several authors who estimate that as many as six of these quadrigae could travel abreast there. Such increasing extravagance cannot be taken seriously anymore, so again, let's move on. In any case, these outer ramparts designed to enclose the city, to absolutely armor-plate it, are backed up by other high walls, just as solid but a little less wide.

At the heart of one of the two sectors of Babylon is the palace of the king; at the heart of the other is a temple devoted to the principal deity and above which a tower supports another tower surmounted by a third tower and so on, up to eight towers girdled by a spiral ramp rising to an oratory furnished with a golden table and a bed. No one spends the night in this bed except, Herodotus is solemnly assured, the principal deity himself in the company of a local woman, but these hearsay stories—the explorer doesn't believe a word of them. As for the great temple of this god, we won't dwell on the tons of gold in its furnishings (throne, pedestal, statues) and the tons of incense burned every year for his festival and the two altars for animal sacrifice—one for young animals, another for older ones—and the huge quantities of offerings given by private individuals: forty liters of wine, fifty liters of flour, forty ewes, every day.

Let's keep going, for it's easy to imagine that Herodotus is exaggerating again about these offerings, unless, having acquired only the barest rudiments of Akkadian, he has not clearly understood what was explained to him during his stay in Babylon. As it happens, these offerings appear on the contrary rather meager when compared to the daily menu prepared, not far away and during the same period, for other local gods (648 liters of barley and spelt for the making of bread, cakes, and pancakes; 648 liters of choice dates, premium dates, dried figs, and raisins; 21 fine barley-fed sheep, 4 milk-fed superlative sheep, 25 ordinary sheep, 2 oxen, 1 suckling calf, 8 lambs, 20 turtledoves, 3 geese, 5 superlative ducks fed on poultry mash, 2 ordinary ducks, 3 duck eggs, and 3 ostrich eggs, all of this washed down with 216 liters of beer and wine) and therefore served, every day, in the temples of Uruk, a city 125 miles to the southeast of Babylon and likewise built on the shores of the Euphrates.

Swift, wide, and deep, the Euphrates cuts Babylon into two sectors in which the straight thoroughfares, running parallel or perpendicular to the river's course on a grid layout, are bordered by houses of three or four stories, the roofs of which, in a country unused to rain, are not made of hard materials. Within the city, the Euphrates flows between high walls and all streets leading to the river gain access to the embankments through portals of the same bronze from which the great city gates were cast. Impetuous as well, capricious, subject to worrying floods, the Euphrates had posed a few problems for Babylon that Herodotus asserts were solved by the two queens Semiramis and Nitocris, one after the other. As for these queens, to begin with, although the reign of Semiramis is a familiar story, one cannot say the same for Nitocris, whose existence is much hazier, even though she is the one in the libretto of Handel's *Belshazzar* who urges the more historically secure Balthazar to consult the prophet Daniel. There also appears to have been a phenomenon peculiar to Babylonian royalty: the queens were said to be the ones who, in male dress, wielded power, controlled construction, and waged war, while a number of effeminate and lazy kings preferred lives of indolence and debauchery, Sardanapalus being the model of this genre.

In any case, as the story goes, first the pugnacious and construction-minded Semiramis had great embankments built on the plain near Babylon to control the flooding of the Euphrates. Later, Nitocris built dikes to make the straight-flowing Euphrates more tortuous—sinuous enough to wind three times past the same village—in order to slow down its waters, confine them to the riverbed, and thus prevent flooding in the countryside. Then Nitocris had a vast artificial lake dug upstream of the city to absorb any overflow from the Euphrates. By chance—or not at all by chance—this lake and these river bends play a defensive role: they complicate the job for neighboring peoples suspected of taking too close an interest in Babylon by prolonging their spies' journeys down the Euphrates, forcing them to take several detours at the end of which they must emerge, exposed to all eyes, upon the lake.

This supposed queen Nitocris, whom Herodotus is perhaps confusing with the wife of Nebuchadnezzar—or even with Nebuchadnezzar himself—took advantage of these projects to also simplify traffic in the city. Since the riverbanks were unstable, folks had to cross from one half of the city to the other by boat, which wasn't always so convenient. So while the queen was diverting the Euphrates to fill up the new lake, thus drying up the riverbed dividing Babylon for a while, she set to work there. She lined the Euphrates's banks within the city and the landing places at the river gates with baked bricks to make the comings and goings of the citizens much easier.

After this, eagerly continuing her urban improvements, Nitocris joined the two halves of the city with a bridge more than a hundred yards long made of stone blocks bound together with clamps of iron and lead—stone blocks she'd had cut during the digging of the lake and brought down from the north, for there is nothing of a mineral nature around Babylon but clay, sand, and mud. Once this work was done, the Euphrates was released into its former bed and the citizens pronounced themselves delighted with this new bridge, of which, for safety's sake, only the piers were made of stone. Again, for safety, square wooden platforms were laid out across these piers during the day and then removed at night so that nocturnal prowlers from the newer western sector could not steal from people asleep in the eastern neighborhoods.

After the Euphrates resumed flowing, river traffic returned to the city. Well, in Babylon, the boats are really unlike any others and they amaze Herodotus, who has never seen the like. And in fact they are round, with neither stem nor stern, and covered all in leather. Constructed in the north, where there are trees, once their framework has been woven of willow branches, sheathed in skins, and those then stuffed with straw, they are launched to float at the mercy of the river. Their main cargo is jars of wine, accompanied by a donkey and two men with paddles standing upright to steer the boat. These boats being of various sizes, Herodotus claims that the largest can carry up to thirteen tons, which seems like a lot. Only another kind of boat, a raft floated by large buoys, can bear such a weight, but the explorer doesn't mention this craft in his notes, in his zeal, perhaps, to astonish his readers with his report of round boats. And when these reach Babylon, the men sell the wine, the straw, the willow wood, and then load the skins on the donkey and walk back home to start all over again.

They doubtless have no trouble selling their wood, for there don't seem to be many trees at all around the city: not the slightest olive or fig tree, not one vine. Only the palm abounds, growing everywhere and serving for everything, providing Babylonians with bread, wine, vinegar, honey, and flour, not forgetting its dates, its heart, and its use in the fabrication of clothing, furniture, pillars, and posts—which explains the Persian song, mentioned by Strabo, celebrating the 360 uses of the palm.

Beyond the plain stretches the sterile desert, dotted with some sort of aromatic bushes and devoid even of the palm but inhabited by all sorts of wild animals one may venture to hunt. Although that isn't so easy: a wild ass, for example, the meat of which is not unlike a more delicate venison, runs faster than a horse, and hunters must chase it in relays to have a hope of bagging one. The too-fleet ostrich is uncatchable, aided in its escape by its wings, which it uses as sails. The bustard is more accessible, for its flight is short and the bird is soon fatigued, but the taste of its flesh is well worth the hunter's own fatigue. (Information furnished by Xenophon, a fellow less given to anecdotes than Herodotus but also less entertaining.)

On the other hand, throughout the alluvial plain surrounding the city and even within its precincts, the soil is wonderfully fertile. Although it rarely rains in this region, the system of irrigation invented by the Babylonians permits a considerable production of cereal crops: barley, several kinds of wheat, and other grains. Herodotus doesn't hesitate to claim that the soil produces up to three hundred times what is sown. He exaggerates, as usual: he knows we know he does that, so, persuaded in advance that no one will believe him, he doesn't bother mentioning just how high the sesame or millet stalks can grow. And it's true that he's been caught, now and then, embellishing certain things: Plutarch figured it would take several books to inventory his lies whereas Aulus Gellius coldly dismisses him as a pathological liar.

But Herodotus doesn't give a damn, coming and going in the meantime, walking about in the streets of the city and its environs, looking all around, gathering information, trying in his clumsy Akkadian to talk with the people he meets, among whom is Tritantaichmes, the satrap of Babylon at the time of his visit, who speaks to Herodotus in particular about the administration of the city. One tries to imagine the explorer taking in this information, inscribing it in his memory before transferring it to papyrus or marking it on clay tablets recto-verso, as the Babylonians do, who keep them as is or, to be on the safe side when the information is important, have them baked.

It is perhaps this Tritantaichmes himself, moreover, whom Herodotus takes as a model to describe the attire of Babylonian men: heavily perfumed, they are shod in the Boeotian style, wear a tunic of linen under another of wool, a light white cloak, a tall headdress like a miter on their long hair, and carry a staff topped with a carved apple, rose, lily, eagle, or some other ornament. And nothing prevents us, either, from imagining this man, dressed in this fashion, deep in discussion with the explorer while having a little beer that one drinks with a straw, as everyone knows they do in Babylon whenever they can and even, eventually—a terra-cotta relief attests to this, preserved in the Musée du Louvre—while having sex.

Speaking of which, there is one Babylonian custom the explorer views with a most critical eye: the requirement that every woman go to a temple to prostitute herself. True, she must perform this duty only once in her life and can then go home, but this system still displeases Herodotus. It displeases him all the more in that it isn't fair: there's a double standard, because while pretty women can swiftly acquit themselves of this task and go on home, this isn't at all the case for the ugly ones, who have a lot of trouble finding a taker and must remain in the temple, sometimes for several years, until they complete their mission. And that Herodotus doesn't like.

He entirely endorses, on the contrary, another institution perfected in Babylon and which concerns marriageable girls. Now this system—he thinks it's perfect. The girls are brought to a marketplace, he explains, to be auctioned off, the prettiest first and then the others in descending order of loveliness, on condition that the buyer marry the one he acquires—with the guarantee that he can return her if they don't get along, and in this case get his money back. Thanks to the funds obtained by the sale of the beauties, handsome dowries are bestowed on the homely ones who are then auctioned off to general satisfaction. It seems, however, that this custom is falling into disuse, which Herodotus thinks is a shame—but it's not impossible that he simply witnessed an ordinary slave auction and didn't understand one iota of it.

The only problem with him is he sometimes goes

too quickly, so that certain developments, certain details vital to the understanding of his story occasionally go missing. And although he may feel these details are of minor interest, he is certainly nowhere near imagining that out of all the contemporary accounts of a trip to Babylon, only his will remain in the history of the world. Were he to imagine this, he might perhaps try at times to be a little more precise, unless, faced with such a perspective, appalled by such a heavy responsibility, he might prefer to drop the whole thing.

Twenty Women in the Jardin du Luxembourg, Clockwise

Saint Bathilde, queen of France, holds in her left hand a manuscript entitled *Abolitio servitutis* and grasps the left edge of her mantle with her right hand. Coiffure: two braids pinned up in the back. Jewelry: a cross pendant. Expression: determined.

Berthe or Bertrade, queen of France, holds a scepter in her right hand and a damaged statuette of a seated man in the palm of her left hand. Coiffure: two very long double braids. Jewelry: nothing to report. Expression: resolute.

Queen Mathilde, duchess of Normandy, holds a

scepter ornamented with fleurs-de-lis in her right hand and with her left grasps the hilt of a sword resting point down on the ground. Coiffure: two braids pinned up in the back. Jewelry: nothing to report. Expression: confident.

Saint Geneviève, patron saint of Paris, crosses her arms at her waist. Her right hand holds a small parchment; the left one grasps the right side of her mantle. Coiffure: two very long asymmetrical braids. Jewelry: a medal pendant. Expression: thoughtful.

Mary Stuart, queen of France, holds a book in her left hand—which is missing two fingers—and in her right she grasps that side of her mantle. Coiffure: curly medium-length hair framing her face. Jewelry: a necklace. Expression: nostalgic.

Jeanne d'Albret, queen of Navarre, holds a stylet in her right hand and a rolled parchment in her left. Coiffure: short curly hair. Jewelry: nothing to report. Expression: inspired. Presence of large breasts.

Clémence Isaure, whose right hand lies on what looks like an armrest and whose left shoulder leans back against a tree trunk, stands with one hip cocked and her raised left hand holding an unidentified object attached to a cord wrapped around her wrist. Coiffure: hair parted down the middle. Jewelry: a two-strand cross pendant necklace. Expression: lost in thought.

Anne Marie Louise d'Orléans, duchess of Montpensier, holds a pair of gloves and a beribboned baton of office in her right hand and graciously extends the left one, allowing a fold of her gown to hang draped over her forearm. Coiffure: hair in ringlets down to her shoulders. Jewelry: nothing to report. Expression: indifferent.

Louise de Savoie, regent of France, points toward the ground with the broken index finger of her right hand, which holds an equally damaged oblong object, and with her left hand slightly raises a fold of her gown. Coiffure: hair pulled back beneath a long head scarf. Jewelry: nothing to report. Expression: imperious.

Marguerite d'Anjou, queen of England, also points the index finger—intact—of her right hand toward the ground, her left arm holding close a child who hugs her, standing on his tiptoes. Coiffure: invisible beneath a complicated headdress. Jewelry: nothing to report. Expression: proud but careworn.

Laure de Noves, whose forearms are crossed over

her abdomen, holds a folded paper in her right hand and the left side of her mantle in her left. Coiffure: short, frizzy curls. Jewelry: a necklace. Expression: resigned.

Marie de Médicis, queen of France, holds a scepter in her left hand and dangles a handkerchief from her right. Coiffure: curly hair puffing out at the temples. Jewelry: nothing to report. Expression: less than amiable.

Marguerite d'Angoulême, queen of Navarre, her left forearm slanting up across her bust, tips her left index finger back just beyond the point of her chin, while the right arm resting along her waist droops at the hand holding a daisy bouquet of four marguerites. Coiffure: short, frizzy curls. Jewelry: a two-strand necklace. Expression: pleasant but affected.

Valentine de Milan, duchess of Orléans, grasps a fold of her gown with her right hand while the left one holds a hefty volume bound with metal fittings, the title of which is partly hidden by her wrist. Coiffure: medium-length hair. Jewelry: nothing to report. Expression: dubitative.

Anne de Beaujeu, regent of France, crosses her arms at her waist, her left hand supporting her right forearm, her right hand prone. Coiffure: invisible beneath the small cap under her crown. Jewelry: nothing to report. Expression: aloof without arrogance.

Blanche de Castille, queen of France, holds in her right hand a long baton leaning against her shoulder; pressed against her waist, her left hand contains a damaged and therefore unidentifiable small object. Coiffure: invisible beneath a crown and head scarf. Jewelry: nothing to report. Expression: distant but dignified.

Anne d'Autriche, queen of France, lets her arms hang by her sides, holding a scepter in her left hand and, partly unrolled in the right one, a parchment bearing the drawing of a building. Coiffure: shoulder-length curly hair gathered into a chignon. Jewelry: nothing to report. Expression: good-natured, a touch bewildered. Presence of large breasts.

Anne de Bretagne, queen of France, holds up both sides of her mantle with her left hand and in her right holds a set of tasseled cords at shoulder height. Coiffure: invisible beneath the small cap under her crown. Jewelry: nothing to report. Expression: stubborn.

Marguerite de Provence, queen of France, whose arms hang slackly over her abdomen, grasps large folds of her mantle in her crossed hands. Coiffure: hair parted down the middle framing her face. Jewelry: a cross pendant. Expression: patient.

Saint Clothilde, queen of France, leaning an elbow on a column, crosses her hands one atop the other at chest height. Coiffure: two very long double braids. Jewelry: nothing to report. Expression: faraway.[1]

CIVIL ENGINEERING

RIGHT AWAY, IN THE ongoing storm, Gluck volunteered to help with the rescue but was given to understand that he might hinder the professional emergency personnel. He soon saw their point and, no longer bothering to wear his hat or use his logo umbrella, he returned to his car in the parking lot near a foundation block at the entrance to the disaster scene. He set out again going north on U.S. Highway 41, where police barriers and diversion signs in the form of enormous blinking arrows were already going up in the opposite direction; he preferred to follow the shore road to the turnoff toward Orlando rather than go more directly to that city via Interstate 75. This would take longer but now he had all the time in the world. To dry his clothes and thinning hair he turned the heat way up, which made the inside of the windshield increasingly foggy until he reached the little town of Ruskin.

Driving along U.S. 41, which supposedly hugs the water but from which one cannot contemplate the bay as one would wish to, Gluck did not try to peer out at beaches, waves, or boats but simply wiped the windshield with a rag from time to time to clear his view of the highway. His staring eyes and contracted features might have indicated an intense effort at reflection, unless they meant a flood of some extreme emotion. Be that as it may, one or the other must have disturbed his proper concentration on driving and he probably realized this, because he stopped for a coffee in the waterfront community of Apollo Beach, at an empty diner called As the Crow Flies, where the rain kept beating, relentlessly, against the windows. After that, when he sat down again behind the wheel, Gluck must not have been any better able to focus on driving the car, a lime-green Chevrolet Caprice Classic convertible a touch too young for him that he'd rented, two days earlier, at the Budget concession at the Orlando Airport. So he simply set the cruise control to take over that decision for him and rested his hands on the wheel, looking vacantly out at the suburban setting cluttered with tourist facilities and blurred by the swishing windshield wipers in this spring of 1980.

Although this scene takes place in the southern United States and there are plenty of people named Gluck scattered around the globe, this particular one pursued university studies in France all the way to the École Centrale des Arts et Manufactures, where he earned a degree in mechanical engineering. Then he got married and took an interest in construction rather than in mines, which were also opening their doors invitingly to him. Quickly joining an agency as a chief engineer, after rising to supervisor he left to establish his own firm where, for twenty-two years, he kept many people working on various civil engineering projects. Most of these involved building bridges, or sometimes dams (which are certainly related to bridges), and at other times tunnels (which are perhaps the opposite of bridges), but anyway mainly bridges, and when his wife died in the winter of 1974, for the next five years Gluck never considered looking for another one.

After the death of Jacqueline Gluck, he sold his

agency for a fine price. He no longer had the heart for building, still less for seducing, so here he is alone now, rich enough and jobless, at leisure for the rest of his days if he likes. A widower no longer attached to anyone or anything, he swiftly realized that basically nothing interested him anymore but bridges. Even though he'd given up building them, he still had to admit that he'd known nothing but them, having devoted all his time, all his attention, and all his thoughts and talents to them. Since abandoning his profession had not changed his taste for bridges, Gluck resolved from then on to devote himself to them alone, to continue and—why not—finish up his life exclusively in their company, without ever needing to leave home. That is how he resolved to tell their life story, a project that at first took the form of "An Abridged General History of Bridges."

Chronologically, it's rather simple. Tired of swinging like a gibbon from tree to tree on a vine, someone had the idea of using this vine for a different purpose and braided those climbing lianas into ropes with which, in order to cross gorges and torrents, we devised the first bridges, properly speaking.

Very quickly, however, experience determined this model to be too fragile and precarious, liable to early wear, and of short life expectancy. So the next inspiration was to bridge such natural obstacles by throwing chopped-down trees across them, simple trunks at first, pruned of their branches, so that one could walk across a chasm without getting too dizzy. (The appearance of vertigo in the history of mankind, by the way, offers much food for thought.) Once all wonder at this tree-trunk inspiration had passed, but taking the trial and error method into account and given the numerous accidents that necessarily ensued, standing balanced on such a bridge was still a major undertaking. Above all it did not allow—as had been promptly anticipated—the transportation of heavy loads, mainly of foodstuffs. So these tree trunks were soon laid in parallel pairs to turn them into a substructure across which smaller logs could be laid, thus giving some breadth to the enterprise: an enrapturing innovation rapidly perfected by using earth and branches to make the logs level.

This was a decisive and most welcome but still insufficient improvement, it was felt, for it restricted the reach of these constructions to the height of a single tree and thus to the necessarily limited length of its trunk. Since the width of certain abysses inconveniently exceeded the size of the oldest oaks, a way of multiplying those dimensions was the next step. This was accomplished through the invention of pilings, designed to support a bridge over water. The piling was first perfected with heaps of rocks tumbled into rivers large or small, followed by stakes driven in a circle into this foundation to make a kind of caisson, itself then filled with boulders. Such supports, placed at intervals across a body of water, permitted folks to line up tree trunks to their heart's content. Now that's progress.

Sometimes, however, up in the colder northern regions, few trees were available. There people turned, for lack of wood, to stone slabs hewn as best they could, until they realized that this substitute material was in fact preferable, much more solid and durable, and put it to general use. But sometimes as well, in the torrid south, few stones were available amid all the sand, so bricks were invented and used first to build temples and palaces, ramparts and ziggurats, and then—quite naturally—bridges. Recourse to brick now offering increased stability and implying new methods of construction, people wound up inventing the arch, some seven thousand years before Gluck. The arch is certainly the best thing we came up with, the thing that would change everything, an invention with which we were by no means finished for there are a few others like that, along the lines of the wheel.

As the first suspension bridges were appearing, along with pontoon bridges made of sampans or barrels lined up and bound together, we began to refine our choice of materials depending on their range of qualities. In the wood department, obviously oak was admirably suited for substructures, alder made excellent posts, while cedar and cypress were best employed in surface construction. As for stone, since tuff had a tendency to disintegrate, travertine burned easily, and marble often had to be imported from far away, a great step was taken with the recourse to mortar. At that point the hardest part was done—and in large part by Rome, until its empire collapsed and the barbarians arrived who, not building anything, destroyed everything they could.

Around 1000 we returned to constructing major roadways, streets, and bridges, all undertaken by a monastic order anxious to rediscover and develop the art of Roman architects. These Bridgebuilding Brotherhoods[1] did not, however, offer much in the way of technical innovation, beyond modifying the form of the arch, from the semicircle to the basket handle and on to voussoirs,[2] while awaiting the Renaissance and the invention of the lattice girder—a structure with a long span composed of compressed elements under tension, a novelty that would also shake things up considerably. After which the serious and methodical leading lights of the Enlightenment would thoroughly reconsider all these acquisitions, before the dawn of a new age of metal.

Helped along by the Industrial Revolution, wood and stone gave way to cast iron. Yet cast iron, ironically, is fragile, tires quickly, and the whole thing ends up cracking, breaking, collapsing over precipices in one catastrophe after another, the worst tragedies in the entire history of bridges until we finally decided to invent steel: robust, resistant, ductile steel. Then came the bright idea of mixing gravel, water, sand, and cement to create concrete, which is a lot less costly than everything else, hard as stone although just as fragile but which comes into its own when reinforced by steel, the two of them now inseparable from then on and voilà.

Thanks to these new materials we began to build new suspension bridges, as in the olden days, except that we dropped the ropes and lianas for helically wound cables or parallel strand cables, sheathed in nylon to avoid corrosion. Attached to pylons by these cables or by heavy rust-proof chains, these suspension bridges were in line to become the longest in the world, their load-bearing capacity allowing them to cross the deepest valleys, the widest estuaries, the mightiest rivers. And while folks were at it, for shorter spans, they thought up the cable-stayed bridge, on which a series of inclined cables supports the weight of the deck, running directly to the pylons in either the harp or the fan design.

At the same time, old models were rethought: cantilever bridges, drawbridges, footbridges and other viaducts and we didn't stop until we'd perfected all that, as much as we could, on an Earth given to quaking a thousand times a day, as everyone knows.

• • •

Having sketched out this first outline of his project and developed it as much as he could, alone in his room, Gluck felt the need to refine, illustrate, and clarify it by going to see these bridges in situ and while he was at it, to finally get out and about. That was three years ago, but for the moment, the rain has calmed down a tad just as he was leaving Spring Hill. Now he will follow the directional arrows that, via Brooksville and Clermont, will guide him to Orlando.

So this is not his first trip, and he has taken a lot of them since he decided to travel the world. These journeys, however, were not begun solely to take his mind off his bereavement: that kind of travel usually goes nowhere, beyond making you go around in circles, for the air's no better far away, you don't feel any freer or more in control or perkier there and there's no end to it. It's even a stretch to tell yourself that you're somewhere far away: for a heady few minutes you see or think you see new things with a fresh eye yet it's a trap, a misunderstanding, because it's not so much a place you're discovering as it is a name you're visiting instead. You feel proud above all about inhabiting it, about tramping around the exotic syllables of this name rather than the panoramas of the place itself, which to be honest swiftly becomes a backwater like any other where you soon think of nothing but going back to the old one, home, when you know perfectly well besides that it's no better there so in short—what was the point.

You should not bestir yourself, therefore, without a goal, an axis, a heading, an idée fixe, otherwise you're better off staying inside your own place looking out. Well, since the only constant thread in Gluck's ideas had always been bridges, it was the project of seeing them that had gotten him going. Bolstered by all his experience, having read all the books, he had therefore decided to visit the greatest possible number of these bridges existent in the world, ideally even all of them although that would be difficult. The bridges, but also of course everything around them and all they overlook: since the type and style of a bridge vary according to the nature of the obstacle it must traverse, the study of that obstacle and its surroundings ought always to be part of the exploration.

This was his modus operandi. He would arrive at a site without ever paying attention to any possible tourist attractions and head straight for the objective. He card-indexed it, photographed it from every angle, examining in detail its setting, the places it joined, the space it spanned; he would cross it in both directions and then leave, and this had been going on for almost three years. His trips to bridges had taken him anywhere there were any and God knows they're everywhere, whether it be above the straits of Kurushima, Messina, the Great Belt and Neko, the gorge of Salgina, the estuary of the Severn, the channel of Kap Shui Mun, Lake Maracaibo, the Bosporus and the Ganges, the waters of the Elbe or the Guadalquivir or the sound that separates the islands of Falster and Farø. Gluck saw them all, having the time and money to do so, now a collector of bridges the way others collect aquatints or bad luck.

He carried a small suitcase containing a change of clothes wrapped around his camera, plus a bound notebook and a memo pad. He stayed in midrange hotels without frills or bedbugs where he didn't try to speak to anyone: the idea never occurred to him. He would spend two days there and in the evenings, up in his room after having supper with a newspaper in the dining room, he'd copy his jottings into his notebook and then good night all, good night all alone. The more bridges he saw, the fewer people he saw, and his mission sharpened his solitude. He never addressed a living soul beyond the hotel staff or, for example, once when his soles wore out, a man selling locally made shoes.

Chronologically scrupulous, Gluck had begun his bridge research with the forerunners of the art, going off to Dartmoor to inspect the first rough-hewn stone constructions made of two uprights capped by a lintel, the Sassanid arches at Kermanshah, the ancient wooden cantilever structures of Nagqu and, at Iwakuni, the scalloped profile of the Kintai-kyo; he surveyed the Pons Augustus and the aqueduct of Segovia before backtracking to take the measure of the Pont du Gard, summarily exhausting the Classic Age, so the hour had come to deal with the constructions of modern times.

He looked. He loved to watch a flash of August lightning fall upon a pylon vibrating proudly like a lightning rod. He loved to see, when the mist had dissolved the tall piers of the Royal Border Bridge, the dark span left floating in the air above the Tweed, and the somber waters of the Potomac reflecting the pale marble arches of the Woodrow Wilson Bridge or, in a narrow passage of the Adriatic, three arid rock islands linked by a trussed thread of a whiteness so like their own that it seemed they'd spun it out themselves. He loved to hear the wind caress a deep chord along a harp of cables or imagine he heard, in a *basso continuo,* the counterpoint of a steel curve on the concrete of a straight viaduct. He loved to count the arches of these structures, which are their successive breaths, creating bridges with varied respiration rates, producing in their reflections on flowing water mobile, trembling sine waves, like those green lines tracing biological cycles one watches on a black monitor at a patient's bedside.

Always impatient to see a new bridge—and sometimes without waiting for it to be finished—Gluck would also eagerly visit work sites around the globe. Just as he had back when he was building bridges, he still liked to see one take shape, watch a suspension cable unrolling in slow motion, tie-cables being attached to the roadway; he liked watching gloved, helmeted, harnessed workers in the heights, rigged out like alpinists or speleologists, checking the anchorage of the suspending rods one by one, and at the end of the assembly he felt deeply moved by the emplacement of the central span between two sections of corbel arch. A professional, he was unbeatable at evaluating the wisdom of choosing this or that girder depending on the site requirements and the purpose of the construction: lattice girder, box girder; narrow and tall or broad and slender; with a rectangular or trapezoidal cross section; an I-beam, T-beam, N-beam, X-beam. He approved or not of the configuration of the cable stays, the symmetry of the masts, the setting of the anchorage blocks. The question of the keystone, separated from the imposts by its haunches, held no secrets for him. He was an expert on the warping of concrete.

Incidentally, while examining every structure, he also took pleasure in locating its breaking point. A point specific to each bridge, a trouble spot hanging in the balance—agreed upon beforehand by the architects in consultation with the local national army for strategic reasons—where a tiny explosive charge would suffice to bring down the entire thing in case of conflict. A point, therefore, both specific and confidential, closely guarded by the military authorities for reasons of national security.

That is how one looks at a bridge, from all its angles and curves, in the spotlight of its future, from its pure profile against a background of clouds to its violent fate among tanks. One could devote one's life to this. One could also tire of it, however, as did Gluck after a few years. Not that he was disenchanted with his mission but, little by little, he began to feel the weight of solitude. Bridges, always bridges; perhaps, in the end, that wasn't a life. When he'd inventoried the ancient structures, the past had still kept him company enough; while inspecting the modern ones, though, he would have liked to share his impressions. He soon began to feel that the thought of looking for another wife, after all that time, would not necessarily offend the memory of Jacqueline who, off where she was, might even approve.

Buoyed by this sentiment, Gluck had therefore resolved to open himself up to the world, to speak to people in hotel corridors and, down in the dining rooms, to try smiling as much as possible. But for a man who for so long had addressed women only to point to a dish on a menu or at shoes in a shopwindow, everyone can agree that this sort of thing doesn't just happen on its own, that seeking a female companion is a surefire way not to find one, that in such an enterprise it's better to be lucky than persistent. Clumsy, lacking experience and method, he'd done his best in vain before giving up. He turned his thoughts elsewhere.

In the early days of 1980, as Gluck was flying to North America to complete his collection, his 747 helped him perceive a fresh parallel. When you get down to it, beyond sharing the privilege of shooting through the air and making sport of altitude, planes and bridges reflect the same mystery, mobile or not, depending, and one that even when explained remains unclear: despite a thousand explications of how an airplane can fly, you'll still think this heavier-than-air plane, even when you're inside it, must be a miracle—and you're not buying it. Same thing with a bridge: engineers can kill themselves showing you the principles of the pier and the beam, the arch and the suspension cable, and you'll still always wonder how it does that, how it hangs on, how it manages to stay up when you go over it.

Having arrived in New York where it was quite cold and where, from the Williamsburg to the Triborough, such puissant mysteries abound, Gluck naturally had his heart set on admiring the Verrazano, the last large suspension bridge built in the country, in 1964, and the world record holder for the longest suspended span. Standing out in the snow during a conversation—initially technical in nature—with a local engineer, Gluck for once eventually touched a bit on his life, the professional side at first, then, gradually, the private one. Indeed, it is better, if you truly want to wax confidential, to do so with perfect strangers, preferably foreign ones because you speak more evocatively of your anguish in a language you haven't mastered, a handicap that drives you straight to the point. Pacing up and down, Gluck had thus described in faulty English his past, his bereavement, the burden of his loneliness, and even the qualifications of a longed-for ideal companion. He had spoken with no expectations, with no other perspective than that presented by the shores of Staten Island, veiled in an icy fog at the other end of the Verrazano-Narrows Bridge. I see, the engineer had said, I understand. Give me your address.

Back in France, Gluck received a letter twelve days later. The engineer had stuck his neck out and alerted a woman of his acquaintance—a little younger than Gluck (although thank god not too much), living in

Spring Hill to the north of Tampa—who, like him, had recently lost a spouse, was just as eager as he to escape her solitude, and whose name was, why not, Valentine Anderson. After sacrificing an entire pad of letter paper, Gluck forced himself to write an acceptable reply before leaving on another trip.

This time he was going to study the site of a future bridge in Sicily, twenty years in the planning and potentially the longest suspension bridge in the world: although the bridge was at risk—situated in a highly active earthquake zone, fought over by architects, hated by local ferryboat companies, coveted by the Mafia—it would one day finally link that island to Calabria. When Gluck got home, he found another letter, with a stamp featuring some pelicans in flight that had been canceled in Palm Harbor and, inside the envelope, a photograph of Valentine Anderson that wasn't bad.

They continued to correspond throughout the winter; then came the spring, which they both thought would be a good season for meeting at last. With this in mind, Gluck examined his travel schedule. He had planned to visit Yugoslavia, this time to attend, at the end of March, the inauguration of the Krk bridge, notable for possessing the longest concrete arch, a new world record he couldn't pass up.

Once the mechanical-doll officers at Krk, in their starred caps and uniforms weighted with several rows of medals, had cut the ribbon for this new bridge, to the accompaniment of the national anthem, "Hej, Sloveni,"[3] in a wind that set their chest medals waltzing and played havoc with the musicians' hair, Gluck took time to admire the interplay of colors of the milk-white arch supporting its chalky deck beneath a Nattier[4] blue sky before he went on home. During the month after Krk, Gluck had intended to visit the Sunshine Skyway Bridge, which he'd never seen and, as it happened, was right in the state where Valentine Anderson lived, so that worked out not too badly.

He made an appointment with her to meet at the bridge on a May morning; they'd each arrive by opposite ends and could rendezvous in the middle. But no, after all: maybe too complicated, meeting there. Fine, let's say at the south entrance to the bridge. In any case that seemed a good idea, certainly a good time of year, because the weather would surely be very lovely the way Florida always is in May.

Civil Engineering

• • •

In the early hours of the morning on May 9, all over Florida, the weather was not looking so lovely after all because a storm had sprung up west of the Gulf of Mexico and begun moving toward Tampa Bay. This disturbance was not exceptionally large, yet it had started producing in its travels enough lightning to make the meteorologists of the coastal stations worry about its electrical strength and decide to take basic precautions.

It was getting close to seven thirty. Captain Ray Bunter, an experienced harbor pilot, had therefore been sent out on his fifty-six-foot *Skimmer of the Sea* to escort the hulking *Summit Venture,* a bulk carrier built four years earlier in Nagasaki. Bunter's job was to guide the cargo ship, designed as a phosphate freighter but sailing empty that day, through the dangerous waters of the bay but especially between the piers of the bridge between Saint Petersburg and Palmetto. As for this bridge, opened in 1954, it was a steel cantilever structure that answered to the name of the Sunshine Skyway even though the sun and sky, for the moment, seemed forgotten by land and sea.

On this bridge, among the stream of vehicles flowing from its northern entrance, a beige Oldsmobile was carrying a man and his dog without either of them noticing behind them, barely visible in the rearview mirror, the white Chevrolet with a black accent stripe. The Chevy, an Impala "bubble top," was advancing to the beat of "One Step Beyond"—covered by the band Madness, 28th on the charts that week—on the car radio and in time to which, on the steering wheel, were tapping the polished nails of Valentine Anderson.

As for Gluck, disappointed by the lousy weather, he was waiting at the south end of the bridge. After flying into Orlando the day before, he had picked up his rental Caprice Classic at the airport, then headed down to Bradenton, where he'd stayed overnight at a Marriott. The darkness of that night was prolonged by that of the storm as Gluck, up early, reached the entrance to the Sunshine Skyway. He drove to some flat ground set up as a parking lot a hundred yards from the bridge and bordered by three shacks. He stayed in his car at first, watching the traffic through the murk; then the drizzle that had fallen since dawn deteriorated into pounding rain, sweeping across the bay in violent and erratic bursts of wind. Before leaving his car, Gluck turned up his coat collar and equipped himself with a hat and umbrella beneath which he made his way to one of the shacks, where he got himself coffee and a dough-nut. After consuming these under the shack's awning, he walked over to the south entrance of the bridge, carrying the umbrella emblazoned with the heat-bonded logo of the Marriott, and began to wait; the rendezvous would be there.

The way Captain Bunter saw it, the *Skimmer of the Sea* was on a routine piloting job. This was hardly his first freighter, no matter what its size. Matchless in his ability to blaze a trail for them in his light craft, he had always known how to guide vessels of the highest tonnage among the shoals of Tampa Bay and the winding bends of its channels. Meanwhile, on the deck of the *Summit Venture,* three men in slickers kept an eye on the marking buoys strategically set out by the crew of the pilot's boat to show where the freighter should turn in the fairway.

With the sky gone black and the sea fading beneath the streaming heavens now raging *rinforzando,* visibility was approaching zero. The ship continued to advance, however, even though the man at the wheel no longer saw anything around him but a vast sheet of rain, while Gluck was having increasing trouble clearly distinguishing the lines of cars that, disappearing onto the bridge, passed those leaving it at a pace steadily weakened by the foul weather. Even the rumbling of car motors was fainter, now confused with that of the battering storm, and horns grew too discouraged to honk.

Through opaque glass furiously swept by long windshield wipers and weeping with condensation inside the cabin, Captain Bunter at his helm suddenly saw looming before him—out of nowhere, almost close enough to touch—a vast dark mass. It was a main pier of the Sunshine Skyway and, driven by winds and currents, he had come upon it much sooner than expected. The captain had time only to shout for engines full astern, but too late. Blindly following in the wake of the harbor pilot—who only just managed to skirt the obstacle—the *Summit Venture* plowed hard into a support piling of the southbound span. The bridge did not immediately react too badly: as the freighter rebounded slightly from the collision before stopping dead in the water, a few chunks of concrete and steel began falling around it, some of them crashing straight onto the bow, where they undertook to damage the sheathing and bash in the deck beams.

Shaken by the impact, the Sunshine Skyway at first kept shedding elements of its superstructure, with girders and beams plummeting and sailing heavily around the vicinity. These black shapes in the gray air were hardly recognizable, massive dark lumps no one had the heart to identify—or the time, either. The noise of their fracture and fall was not yet clearly discernable, amid the clamor of the churning waves and howling wind, but when the support pier began to collapse, it did so in a violent concert of erratic booms and snapping ruptures, vicious screeching and deep groans amplified by an avalanche of braces, traverse beams, spacers, pieces of metal as sharp as a guillotine blade and bolts the size of baby carriages.

These details would disintegrate into a major uproar, a chaotic choir, an industrial din fusing together all individual material wails when—desperately bent to the limit of its resistance—a monumental stretch of roadway collapsed into the bay. For with the gigantic clamor of a monster wounded to the death, with polyphonic cries of horror and chagrin, suffering and fury, that area of the southbound span came apart in two phases.

The fall of a first section had tumbled six cars, a pickup, and a Miami-bound Greyhound bus 165 feet into the water. A second section of the roadway held on shakily for forty seconds while, alone at the precipice within a yard of the edge, there remained only the beige Oldsmobile with the man and his dog, and behind them, the white Impala bubble top with the black stripe. In the fierce wind and blinding rain, these vehicles had just reached that part of the bridge when it began to shake bizarrely. With zero visibility, however, the drivers attributed the phenomenon to the weather and kept going, but staring automatically at the windshield, the driver of the Olds abruptly saw a freighter straight down in the bay while there now seemed to be, between him and this freighter, nothing. Stunned at the sight and by the quaking of the roadway, he slammed on the brakes and began to leave his car, advising his dog to do likewise. When the dog refused to follow him, the man made the mistake of hesitating a moment while the roadway started heaving even more frenetically. Then it was the whole world that began to seesaw: more suspending rods had given away, dropping that part of the span and all it carried, flinging the Oldsmobile with the man and his dog and Valentine Anderson's Impala bubble top through the air. Respectively, they performed a double and a triple salto through gray space before landing right on the *Summit Venture,* rebounding heavily off its bow to go sink thirty feet into the bay, as the interior of the Chevrolet rocked to the beat of "Upside Down" sung by Diana Ross—and that song, that week, was number nineteen on the hit parade.

Down in the fog where he was, in his corner of the parking lot under the downpour, Gluck was not able to see that all these vehicles, having kept their windows closed on account of the weather, were not immediately swallowed up by the bay. Resurfacing for a few seconds in the crossfire of waves, as if in limbo, they floated a while thanks to their air bubbles, just long enough for the other songs playing on the other radios to end and then, slowly, they went under.

Gluck started his car, maneuvered his way out of the lot, and disappeared in the direction of Orlando and, seven years later, the bridge was replaced by a more solid structure with a cable-stayed main span in the fan design. To make it more visible in all kinds of weather, care was taken to paint it in a livelier color: covering the 435 miles of its cables required three thousand gallons of yellow paint.

NITROX

LET'S TAKE FOR EXAMPLE, sitting in an empty and cubi-cal cell of carceral appearance, a young woman named Céleste Oppenheim. She consists of a lovely tall person wearing her black hair in a pageboy, with an indiffer-ent expression but a penetrating gaze, while her face and figure are striking enough to arouse the immedi-ate interest of absolutely any casting or commercial and fashion modeling agency. A figure all the more riveting, by the way, in that Céleste Oppenheim happens at the moment to be wearing only a white bra and panties, there being no other clothing lying around on the fur-niture since there is no furniture here, neither chair nor table nor storage unit, only a bed, or more precisely, a couchette bed.

This scanty clothing does not seem to bother the young woman because it is ferociously hot in the no-frills, vapid, windowless cube with sweating bare yellow walls. Poorly illuminated by two neon ceiling fixtures, one of them crackling, the cube is equipped with an outsize radiator that explains all this heat, a washbasin, and that metal couchette bed, a single: rusty, reduced to a bedstead bolted to the floor, covered with a pad of polyurethane foam crumbling at the corners and at one end of which lies a bedspread with gray and beige motifs, folded in six, the other end being at present sat upon by Céleste Oppenheim. The latter shows no emotion when the cell door slides open to reveal two men of about forty: dressed alike in cotton duck pants of the same faded blue and sou'westers (one a candied chestnut color, the other bottle green, both embroidered on the left arm with an insignia in red silk), the men could just as well be two associates as an official with his underling.

Without speaking or entering, from the threshold they beckon the young woman, who next finds herself in a sort of storeroom, a large, dimly lit space apparently warehousing bags, crates, chests, and other boxes.

Making their way among these containers they come to a small open area where, hanging from a rack, is an outfit composed of rubber and metal devices including a mask and flippers. Candied Chestnut indicates to Céleste Oppenheim that she should put all this on, while Bottle Green speaks up politely to warn her that what comes next will not be a piece of cake. His defective elocution, however, as fuzzy as a poorly tuned radio, prevents the young woman from following this speech while she is dressing, distracted as she already is by the complexity of the outfit as well as by her relief—probably—at no longer finding herself just about naked in front of two male strangers. Of the man's stammered cautions, she basically catches only the words *prudence* and *pressure,* that last apparently the main object of his warning.

Once the young woman has donned this equipment, Candied Chestnut hands her a Btex polyester bag with huge zippered pockets while guiding her toward another sliding door, through which she passes to find herself in a new cell much like the other one. The difference being that this one is even more empty, distinctly more humid, and neither heated nor lighted at all, devoid of the slightest furnishing and at the far end of which, exactly matching the shutter about to be locked behind her, Céleste Oppenheim has barely time to glimpse, straight ahead, another closed door. A few seconds later, she hears jets of water hissing all around her in the dark, more and more powerfully until she soon feels her calves, thighs, waist, and then her chest submerged. As soon as the water reaches her shoulders, she lowers the mask to cover her face and waits for the door in front of her to rumble open.

When it has and Céleste Oppenheim is completely underwater, the young woman stretches out horizontally in the prone position and glides through the opening into more blackness. Turning on a large flashlight extracted from one of the bag's zippered pockets, she inspects her new environment: nothing remarkable at first glance in this icy opacity. Before getting her bearings, she turns to look at the dark contour of the submarine from which she has just emerged and which hovers as she does at a depth of about eighty feet, subjecting her, as Bottle Green had said, to three and a half bars of pressure—one of atmospheric pressure while the other two and a half are hydrostatic.

The sub in question is a small one, modeled after

the Aurore class of submarines (Q200) built in Nantes between 1945 and 1960 at the Dubigeon shipyard, but twice as small, about a hundred feet long and drawing thirteen feet of water, able to descend to a depth of 330 feet thanks to its diesel-electric propulsion system and as it sinks toward the abysses swimming with increasingly blind and ugly fish, the young woman sees only a teardrop silhouette, a pale blackfin tuna on a darker black backdrop.

The flanks of submarines being rarely supplied with windows, no familiar yellow glow framed—why not—by cretonne curtains sends out any reassuring signal. For a moment the submersible's expressionless albacorean profile may be glimpsed, diminishing as they each go their own way, and Céleste Oppenheim rapidly finds herself all alone at the bottom of the sea. As her eyes gradually adjust to this biotope, she begins to distinguish a bit of flora, a bit of fauna traversing the flashlight beam from time to time. Among the daphnia and sponges she encounters a bevy of moonfish, a few jellyfish of the *Linuche* or the pelagic kind, and a member of the "knit-striped" sea snake family. Not far away must roam dugongs and manatees, sharks, rays, and chimaeras[1]—all creatures that would tell an expert that she is somewhere in a marine environment of the Indo-Pacific. Opening another pocket of her Btex bag, Céleste Oppenheim pulls out a square sheet of plastic printed with contours, axes, and coordinates.

After studying it a moment, then correcting a particular angle of her horizontal progression, the young woman follows her itinerary until she reaches an area of irregular relief which—albeit informed in advance of its position by the plastic document but noticing it only at the last moment—she almost bumps into and which forms a kind of hill or even mountain beneath the waves. Fairly certain of the zone she must now be in, she stops swimming to look around for a peak marked on the diagram, a kind of column supposedly right next to the hill: this is her objective, and it takes her a few minutes to find it.

It is, in fact, a sort of thick obelisk of an irregularity too evident, too decisive to be a natural phenomenon, and its long strands of red, green, and brown seaweed, the eel grass and *Spirogyra,* the *Lithophyllon* and *Tricleocarpa* colonies that carpet its flanks disguise its man-made origin rather clumsily—but it's true that the place isn't overrun with people wondering about its origins. Having identified this protrusion, Céleste Oppenheim begins to circle it, scrutinizing every inch of its surface until she finds what she's looking for: a circular hole about the diameter of a bicycle wheel, apparently the entrance to a pipe it would be appropriate to enter.

Hardly has she done so when this opening closes like the diaphragm of a camera, the iris of curved leaves converging upon the center to overlap themselves into closure, and she keeps swimming until she bumps into the end of the narrow tube. There she remains immobile, cloistered in this new lock chamber that gradually begins to empty itself of water until it's dry, when the far end opens and light appears at last, toward which Céleste Oppenheim now starts to crawl.

At the other end of this tunnel she must somehow turn herself around to get out. After taking off her flippers, which she places in a net bag, she manages to step backward onto the top rung of a ladder, which she descends. Regaining the open air in a huge and quite brightly lighted hangar, the half-blinded young woman has to blink repeatedly until her eyes are used to this new environment. As high as it is wide and constructed on several levels, with dividing walls that intersect via stairs and passageways, this hangar is furnished with machines no less cumbersome than they are unidentifiable, while part of its ground floor is a parking lot for carefully lined-up underwater scooters. Wearing striped fluorescent outfits, a number of people are busy everywhere, carrying and silently shifting things, consulting blueprints, apparently paying no attention to the young woman.

And she, for a while, contemplates this new setting without taking off the rest of her accoutrements, without even removing her mask, through the "window" of which I can make out her blank expression, watching her from my armchair in my office a few yards from the tunnel exit and separated from the general area by another window, this one of two-way glass, naturally.

Then I see her strip off her equipment, unbuckling her mask before taking off her weight belt, her stabilizer vest, diving regulator, Btex bag, and tank of Nitrox, a mixture of enriched air prescribed for such depths. Freed from these accessories, Céleste Oppenheim is now wearing nothing but her charcoal-gray neoprene wet suit, appealingly skintight, to my great delight. I see her rummage once more in one of those zippered pockets, emptying it of a few technical accessories—the flashlight, the dive map—but also pulling from a different pocket various cosmetic accessories, a comb along with a small mirror, and I watch her apply makeup, discreetly giving her face a bit of color, in little dabs, before the indifferent eyes of my employees.

I light a cigarette and take the time to smoke the whole thing—which is even more strictly forbidden in a submarine habitat but, by now it's obvious, I am the boss here—while enjoying this show before rising and leaving my office to join her. I head over to Céleste who hadn't noticed me right away but smiles when she recognizes me; I usher her toward my office and when we're finally alone, I happily open my arms to her, holding her close, brushing my lips over the neoprene all the more pleasurably in that I'm very fond of the taste of salt—indeed I'm often reproached for that, I always oversalt my food.

Three Sandwiches at Le Bourget

ON THE FIRST SATURDAY in the month of February, having gone to bed quite late the previous evening, I arose quite late as well and decided to go have a sandwich in Le Bourget. This resolution was something I'd been mulling over for a while.[1]

Walking toward Gare du Nord, I was almost diverted from my purpose, in particular when passing the front windows of a pizza-by-the-slice place on Rue de Maubeuge* and then the kebab seller's shopwindow on Rue de Dunkerque,* but I didn't give in. I held out. Nothing could be allowed, despite my hunger, to interfere with my project.

At Gare du Nord I got lost for a moment in the station trying to get to the RER B, one of the five rail lines in the Réseau Express Régional serving Paris. It was not my habit to go to Le Bourget, in fact it was the first time I was attempting to go there, for reasons too long to explain. So I had never gone there. I didn't know anyone there. I had nothing to go see there. A few escalators weren't working, that threw me off, but in the end I found the entrance to the Réseau, then spotted a ticket vending machine, from which I obtained a round-trip ticket (I had no intention, either, of hanging around Le Bourget forever), taking advantage without any hesitation of the reduction available with a senior citizen card.

I felt some pride in swiftly and efficiently completing this self-service purchase even though, through clumsiness, I dropped a few coins, which forced me to crouch down to get them, which I don't like doing and neither, I would imagine, do most other people with senior cards.

When I got on the train, there weren't too many of us; a young man was sitting across from me. Through my window I watched an endless perspective of the tags and graffiti, sometimes in palimpsest, that fill the vast majority of the walls along the tracks. I pulled my notebook from my pocket (a small, oblong, beige notebook from New York, witness the price tag: BOB SLATE STATIONER $1.10) and considered writing them down but there were too many; I couldn't manage to decipher them all and anyway other people must already have done that long before me.

As I was coming to that conclusion, the young man across from me asked where I was going. Le Bourget, I told him. With a look of concern, he informed me that I must have taken the wrong train, this one being a nonstop express to the terminus, Mitry. When I asked him if it was far, Mitry, he led me to understand that it was in fact quite far, that I was in something of a predicament; he even mimicked the gesture of a desperate fellow making an emergency phone call for help. While I was reassuring him, intimating that it wasn't serious and I had plenty of time, he began to laugh, saying no, it was a joke, and he asked what time it was. I told him: twenty past two. That's when the train stopped at the first station: La Plaine-Stade de France. We didn't say much after that; the young man got off at the next station, La Courneuve-Aubervilliers,* after wishing me good day rather coolly, which didn't seem to jibe with his practical joking, and that's when some light hail began to fall, as I watched, on the platforms of that station. I'd brought along no hat, no umbrella, no nothing.

When the train left again, I kept watching out the window and saw what was left of the Mécano factory (the lettering of that name reminded me of the one for those old toys, Meccano); then came other companies that seemed more active, especially one involving industrial packaging, until the train stopped at the next station, Le Bourget, my destination. Getting up to get off, I encountered three young guys standing by the doors listening to rap on their cell phones. I glanced at them; they gave me a look with no love lost but that's fine, that's fine.

It was now raining at the station, a chilly little drizzle, rather hostile, and I went into the Hôtel de la Gare, which is also a bar and brasserie, just across the way, between the station pharmacy and a medical analysis laboratory. I found a table near the picture window and sat down; there weren't too many of us there, either. Across from me, the train station at Le Bourget was architecturally reminiscent of an old inexpensive construction set (which reminded me again, by association, of the Meccano toys); three buses were parked in front of it. A big sign described the project currently underway to permit the RER B to link up with a future line called Tangentielle Nord. I waited for a bit.

A man finally showed up, from whom I ordered a ham-and-gruyère sandwich and a glass of Côtes du Rhône: my project was taking shape. Outside, people were going by with umbrellas, visored caps, hoods, shawls, knit caps—one with a pom-pom—but I had nothing like that. The sandwich arrived with its glass of red. I couldn't really say if they were good, I rather think they weren't particularly but that wasn't the point.

In that establishment, as on the sidewalks outside, were plenty of West Indian, North African, and sub-Saharan men and women, as well as a few Asians but not so many as that, and not just them. I did intend to buy an umbrella but I wasn't sure I'd find one in the neighborhood around the station—and umbrellas, in any case, I already had several at home, all in rather poor working order, which reminded me of the one hundred umbrellas found in Erik Satie's[2] house after his death, out in Arcueil where, incidentally, I could have gone directly afterward by taking the same RER B in the opposite direction but, later, later. Some other time, perhaps.

As often happens at a Hôtel de la Gare, a radio was endlessly playing golden oldies. I recognized without too much trouble Paul McCartney singing "Michelle" while a guy and two girls at a neighboring table animatedly discussed long-term contracts, vacations without pay, and the status of temps. The sun came back out for a moment: disappearance of umbrellas, rarefaction of headgear. On that note I finished my sandwich and drained my glass: mission accomplished.

Before leaving the Hôtel de la Gare, I had time to watch the conversion of a try after thirty minutes of play in a rugby match on the television wall-mounted not far from the bar (Ireland 20, Wales 0). Above this bar, as it happened, a rugby ball was on display along with four soccer balls outfitted, just for a laugh, with different caps (I recognized one from the French national railroad) and a dark blue beret of the Naval Fusiliers.

Afterward, I went for a walk in the town. I went along Avenue Francis-de-Pressensé,* lined with low pebble-dash buildings and classic detached houses of brick or buhrstone like the ones often found in suburbs and, even more often, in descriptions of those suburbs. I noticed one of the ubiquitous Bar de l'Europe cafés on the avenue, as well as two Stars: a Star of Istanbul (bar-restaurant-grill) and a Golden Star (butcher shop). I turned left onto Avenue Jean-Jaurès,* which featured the bar-brasserie-tobacconist L'Aviatic. Not far away, practically across the street, was a bookshop-news-stand-stationery store where the front window was entirely filled with all kinds of models and figurines including a gigantic representation of Nefertiti in the round. I wondered what she was doing there. Having subsequently learned that the lady running that establishment had been mugged several times by youths professing some sort of allegiance to Islam, I wondered if that recourse to Nefertiti might be a vaguely metonymic way of warding off those nuisances.

There were also quite a few fast-food establishments on the avenue (numerous places featuring Turkish, Pakistani, Indian, or Sri Lankan dishes), a few halal or not butcher shops, a few hairdressing and beauty salons including a black-and-white Cosmétique and a black Beauté, plus all sorts of the usual stores such as a jeans emporium, wellness and beauty center, florist, locksmith, Franprix, and Leader Price.

Then I dawdled awhile on Avenue de la Division-Leclerc,* site of the city hall (entirely of brick) and the building housing police headquarters. The latter must have once been the home of a leading citizen: vaguely châteauesque in inspiration, beige and salmon pink, with a pointy pinnacle turret and a roof protected by four lightning rods—which seemed a touch much, and I thought the police could have recycled them as antennas. A sort of yellowing palm was hanging on in front of the façade, from which drooped an astonishingly faded French flag. All shutters were closed save one, on the ground floor, open just a crack. This time I debated whether this institution might be viewed as sealed up tight like a citadel or simply closed for the weekend. Directly across the avenue, a young woman dashed out of a grocery store and into a double-parked car, calling out to me, Hey monsieur, I can buy you a drink if you want. I didn't really know what that implied; I preferred not to be too sure of what her words meant, or even very sure in fact that she was addressing me (although I don't see whom else she could have been addressing, I do believe there was no one else at that moment and on that rather empty bit of sidewalk whom she could have called monsieur), but in any case I opted for not answering.

True, I have to say that I was wearing a pair of dark glasses I'd pulled from my pocket when the sun had come out again. Now, perhaps it was incongruous to be wearing dark glasses in Le Bourget in early February, maybe that could seem like a kind of provocation, a vague social class marker as it appears to have been in 1960, in Créteil, if the Jean Ferrat song that sprang to my mind can be believed.[3]

The sky clouded over again, though, and thinking it might rain once more I repocketed my dark glasses while returning to the station (which by now seemed almost familiar) and, on platform 2B, I had not long to wait for my train home. This time the car was full and I traveled standing. The banal but always intriguing idea occurred to me that all these people had, every one of them, a good reason for traveling, and that mine had been merely that sandwich in Le Bourget.

Five days later, I decided to renew it, that reason, slightly improved. This time I would further refine two aspects of the plan: firstly, a specific destination in Le Bourget, and I rapidly selected the bar-brasserie-tobacconist L'Aviatic, previously noticed and to whose face, if I may say so, I'd felt immediately drawn; secondly, the nature of the sandwich, and here I chose the salami sandwich. That's a quite common kind of sandwich, such a classic in France that it's familiarly known as a *sec-beurre* [4] but which seems to me, over the past few years, to be appearing less often on menus, to be less desired by consumers, so that one might wonder about a possible tendency for the rate of *sec-beurre* popularity to decline.

Desirous of putting this hypothesis to the reality test while evaluating the capacities of L'Aviatic in this respect, I thus set out again for Le Bourget five days later, having this time—for experience, as we know, influences method—equipped myself with a cap.

I'd hardly set out for Gare du Nord when a sentence popped into my mind that I thought sounded not bad: I stopped to write it down in my notebook (this time it was a slightly bigger one, printed by the Museo de Arte Moderno de Medellín, and I haven't the slightest idea where I could have gotten it since I've never set foot there). Now, this sentence, aside from being all in all not so terrible, was certainly false, even mendacious. And I was doubtless punished for this lie by my ballpoint pen which, bridling in protest, energetically refused to write it. I shook the pen in vain in every possible direction: it was on strike. I had to accept that it was out of ink and make a big detour over to the stationery store on the corner of Avenue Trudaine* and the Rue Rodier to buy a new cartridge.

I could have bought a new ballpoint, it wouldn't have cost me any more than the cartridge, but I was fond of my pen, I'd grown attached to it: I admired its rocket- or torpedo-like silhouette, its ingenious safety clasp, its prettily combined materials (brushed metal, shiny metal, plastic), plus it felt good in the hand and the slogan "I (heart) NY" suggested that it had come from the same place as my beige notebook, and it wasn't very handsome but I was fond of it. Also it was practical for taking notes while walking, given its retractable tip, so it was more practical than the Pilot V5 Hi-Tecpoint 0.5 mm I usually use, but its cap, which must be removed then put back on (and where do you put it in the meantime), slows everything down.

Anyway, good thing I'd brought along my little cap because it was going to rain, although lightly and briefly but let's not get ahead of ourselves. This time the train was neither empty nor full. I took a jump seat. First facing the back of the train (as I usually do in the métro) then facing forward for a better view of the landscape.

And what more did I notice than on last Saturday? A tower topped with the name Siemens, a canal, a beautiful big factory in ruins, companies I found apparently in working order (the industrial packaging one, already noted, was next to an iron- and steelworks, but there were also, for example, the ham company Jambon Georges Chanel and Transports Henri Ducroc), an immense number of buildings one wouldn't necessarily want to say were inhabited, a soccer field where some youths were playing, a vast zone of trash from which arose smoke as if from shantytown chimneys—and perhaps that was the case: I promised myself vaguely that I would check up on that one day.

After arriving at the Le Bourget station, just when I saw the pharmacy and was feeling on familiar terrain, my ballpoint broke down again. This time it was the spring mechanism that had jammed like any old Colt .45 and, to my great surprise, standing on the platform, I fixed it myself. I would never have thought I could do it. I resolved to handle it more delicately from then on.

It was too early, I wasn't hungry enough to settle that business of the sandwich at L'Aviatic—too early even to eat without being hungry: I decided to go for a walk. First, under the pretext of buying a daily paper, I dropped by the bookshop-newsstand-stationery store. Probably for reasons already mentioned, the entrance was locked up tight like a jewelry store: I had to ring the doorbell to be let inside. Then I spent considerable time looking for the publication I wanted, a mildly left-wing daily of which a single copy turned up on the bottom shelf of the display unit, almost invisible, whereas all the extreme-right papers were throwing out their chests in the place of honor. This sight annoyed me. I reconsidered my hypothesis regarding Nefertiti.

Then, at something of a loss while waiting for sandwich time, I turned onto Avenue de la Division-Leclerc.

Lots of places were either closed, not long for this world, or seriously dilapidated, and with a gray sky overhead it wasn't cheerful. Even though it would sabotage my plans for L'Aviatic, after a while I considered dining somewhere else but the only establishments that would have seemed worthy of consideration—Le Moderne and L'Étoile-Diamant—looked deserted (L'Étoile-Diamant, in particular, with its ashtrays on the floor and its chairs tipped over in all directions, appeared to have been abruptly closed at the height of a general brawl). I walked. I passed three kids leaving their school who were working hard at improvising jingles on scatological themes. Maybe because of the overcast weather, the intermittent rain, this whole environment was giving me a rather sad, rather impoverished impression, and as I was passing another newsstand, when I saw the front-page question on *Les Échos*—"Can One Still Become Rich in France?"—that question, in situ, seemed well founded. I was similarly interested, from another point of view and on the other side of the avenue, by this sticker on the back window of a charcoal gray Mercedes 300D: "Love for all, hatred for none"—a worthwhile idea at first glance although perhaps a trifle awkward to implement. I kept on walking.

I walked to the town of Le Blanc-Mesnil, far enough to glimpse in the distance the two launch rockets Ariane 1 and Ariane 5, spires marking the site of the Musée de l'Air et de l'Espace. As I was crossing the overpass spanning the Autoroute du Nord, bristling with antinoise barriers, Avenue de la Division-Leclerc turned into Avenue du 8 Mai 1945* before recovering its old name of Route de Flandre a little farther, toward the northeast. I tried to get as close as I could to those rockets, which strangely became harder and harder to see the nearer I got, but I put off my visit to the museum for another day. I was in no rush. Besides I was now seriously hungry.

Betraying L'Aviatic, I spotted an establishment of the truck stop kind called Au Bon Accueil. I went in this "Welcome Inn" and was in fact not too badly received; I sat at the bar, the hostess was a pleasant blonde and rather pretty, which cheered me up. When I asked without much hope if there might, by any chance, be a possibility of having a salami sandwich—I was still following, obviously, a certain train of thought—I was quite startled to hear the prompt riposte: plain or garlic? Disconcerted by such variety, in my flusterment I forgot to consider the possibility of a cornichon option, but now that I think back on it, I feel sure that would have worked. So I simply replied plain. With a glass of red. (This glass had become a deliberate imperative, even a compulsion that I will not have the cheek to qualify as a matter of style.) While awaiting my order, I discreetly observed my neighbors at the bar: two men drinking beer were followed by two men drinking *kirs*. Hardly any truck drivers remained, I felt, among the clientele, who seemed more like employees of the nearby airport or of security or property-caretaking companies—at least that's what I thought I could deduce from reading the writing on the backs of their jackets. I ate my sandwich while glancing through my newspaper.

I then decided to stroll back to the station without any rush, tracing the same route, taking care only to avoid using the same sidewalks, for a fresh point of view, which allowed me to take a closer look at the police station building than I'd gotten the other day: this time three windows (out of ten) were open. Definite progress.

To take the edge off my betrayal, I dropped by L'Aviatic after all for coffee. Next door was the Cinéma Aviatic, a defunct movie theater, worse than defunct, like a carcass left to rot without burial. On the blind wall of its façade, traces yet remained of poster frames, remnants of words; the doors had been walled up and over them hung torn posters advertising musical and sportive entertainments. High on this rectangular surface, the only opening—at one time the projectionist's window for fresh air, perhaps—was plugged with a colorful but moldy old blanket. This wall was clearly no longer a good place to lean while waiting for the 152 bus.

And yet, everything had gone well for this movie theater at first. Named for its proximity to the airport, L'Aviatic had opened between two wars: behind a splendid façade decorated in bas-relief, huge crowds packed an immense theater seating twelve hundred and which, thirty years later, was renovated for the projection of 70-millimeter films and which, ten years later, had been demolished to make way for a three-theater complex and which, twenty years later, had shut its doors forever and which, today, bought up by the adjacent brasserie of the same name, was now in a state of such abandonment that one felt like crying: *histoire du cinéma.*

Meanwhile, along the same sidewalk as the police station, I had also passed the church. It seemed to me quite difficult to talk about Le Bourget's church, consecrated to Saint Nicholas; difficult, because one wouldn't want at all to seem unkind. But it had to be said that it was a crummy church, really crummy, so crummy that it became touching. Very discreet and almost unassuming, it even seemed so conscious of its ugliness that one could feel nothing but affection for it.

When I drew nearer, to my extreme surprise I saw affixed to the left of the church entrance an official sign proclaiming it a historic monument. At first I wondered through what string pulling, influence peddling, and dark machinations such a homely building had managed to be thus classified, obtaining that prestigious designation—until I learned that it had seen quite an eyeful, this church. Like the Cinéma Aviatic, it had had its adventures: built in the fifteenth century, dedicated to Saint Nicholas in the sixteenth, fallen into ruin and demolished two hundred years later, rebuilt then remade into a Temple of Reason under the Revolution, dedicated to the Supreme Being by the Convention,[5] pillaged in 1815,[6] bombarded during the War of 1870[7] (during which it served as a fallback position for French and Prussian soldiers in alternation—witness the bullet damage to the tympanum over the church door), reconstructed two years before the one of '14, the church had well deserved a bit of a breather and, quiet at last, to achieve the title of monument. But it was closed. One couldn't go inside. Its fate moved me. I phoned the curé.

That is how on the following Sunday—the fifth Sunday in liturgical Ordinary Time—I went to Mass at Saint-Nicolas du Bourget, along with my ballpoint pen and Colombian notebook. It was extremely cold and, out the train window, what did I now see that I hadn't seen before? A mushroom-shaped water tower, a bulk paper recycling plant (where, I happened to reflect with some melancholy, this notebook might end up): not much, actually. But above all I was able to verify that what I had taken for a slum was one, in fact, right by the headquarters of Paprec, a leader in the collection, recycling, and valorization of waste—and of that proximity, make what you will.

So having arrived at Le Bourget, I went directly to the church and along the way I spotted a stela that had until then escaped my notice, standing in front of the community center. It was a stone parallelepiped, carved with palms and a broken sword, with this inscription at its base (capital letters and Roman numerals):

Bourget October 30 December 31 1870
They died to defend the fatherland
The sword of France broken in their valiant hands
Will be forged anew by their descendants

I went on my way.

The church was almost full, a good half of those present being African or West Indian, or Guyanese, perhaps. The five paintings decorating the side walls presented grim episodes of the Franco-Prussian War, one of which was set inside the church itself, with a toppled confession booth in the background. In bellicose echo, the altar decorated with what must be described as incrustations bore only two inscriptions, the dates 1914 and 1918—because there is more to life than 1870. Three figures stood there, as they often do: Joseph, John the Baptist, and Mary. She, in bas-relief, appeared here as Our Lady of the Wings, protectress of aviators, in homage to the town's aeronautical past. She had wings like an angel and—doubtless to fly even faster—was framed as if in parentheses by two big plane propeller blades, one of them rather primitive (frankly, rather board-like), and the other more classically shapely. As for the rest, the stained-glass windows weren't terrible, being vaguely coloristic abstractions of the kind popular in the mid-nineteenth century, while near the ceiling five (out of ten) heaters barely of more recent vintage seemed to be in working order. They labored somewhat in vain, actually, functioning so little that I couldn't stay there more than forty-five minutes, I was so cold, but still I did wait until the end of the homily. It was well done, the homily, typical but well done.

Leaving the church, I was almost as hungry as I was cold, but, no sandwich on the horizon. A winter Sunday, late morning, northeastern suburb: empty streets, few passersby, even establishments still ordinarily open were closed. Giving up on my sandwich, I turned right, heading back toward the station and walked to the cemetery at a brisk pace in an attempt to get warm. The cemetery was farther away than I'd have thought and I even almost lost heart but I persevered. I found it, I went in and I was all alone there when, after a few moments, no: I saw a lady appear in the distance with a watering can. Like the church and the entire town, the cemetery bore definite signs of having been affected by both war and aviation, sometimes in combination: the graves of soldiers and pilots, funeral plaques showing images of medals, busts topped with helmets or kepis.

The place wasn't too bad, but soon a few broken and gaping tombs—I'd never seen such a thing—began to make me feel uncomfortable. I didn't venture to peer inside their dilapidation, I walked away. Then I noticed a full-size statue of a soldier in the war of 1870. Its face half corroded by erosion, it had unwillingly become a frightening effigy of the *gueules cassées*[8] of the following war, men with monstrously disfigured faces, and there, beneath that icy sky, something like a sickening feeling came over me: I left without looking back. I went toward the station and tried to think about what I was going to have to eat. On the way to the train I saw hardly anyone. The church, by that time, must have been empty. L'Aviatic was deserted. Police headquarters was all shut up. And this cemetery, in the end, was of hardly any interest save that—not so slight—of being ingeniously located on an extension of Rue de l'Égalité, where equality is extended to everyone.

CREDITS

These stories, now slightly modified, were published in the following works or periodicals.

Marie-Paule Baussan provided the idea behind "Nelson": *Le Garage*, no. 1, 2010.

"The Queen's Caprice" ("Caprice de la reine") was written for Jean-Christophe Bailly: *Les Cahiers de l'École de Blois*, no. 4, January 2006.

"In Babylon" was commissioned by William Christie and Les Arts Florissants to mark their recording of Handel's oratorio *Belshazzar* in October 2013.

"Twenty Women in the Jardin du Luxembourg, Clockwise" is included in Sophie Ristelhueber's *Le Luxembourg*, Paris-Musées, 2002.

Credits

An extract from "Civil Engineering" was sent to Patrick Deville, literary director of the Maison des Écrivains Étrangers et des Traducteurs de Saint-Nazaire, and appeared in a bulletin of that organization's international writers' symposia: *meeting*, no. 4, 2006.

"Nitrox" was published in *Tango,* no. 1, May 2010.

"Three Sandwiches at Le Bourget" took shape in the context of a theatrical project in 2014, stemming from a suggestion by Gilberte Tsaï.

NOTES

Nelson

1. The War of the Second Coalition (1799–1802) was waged by the conservative European monarchies (led by Britain, Austria, and Russia) against revolutionary France, where Napoléon had taken charge as first consul late in 1799. When Russia pulled out to form the League of Armed Neutrality with Denmark-Norway, Sweden, and Prussia, the British saw this as a threat to their naval supremacy and vital trade advantages. On April 2, 1801, Vice Admiral Horatio Nelson led the main attack in the first Battle of Copenhagen against a Danish-Norwegian line anchored just off the city, and after an extremely hard-fought engagement, he carried the day. Command of the British fleet was transferred to Lord Nelson, who became Viscount Nelson of the Nile. In March 1802, Britain and France signed the Treaty of Amiens, temporarily ending hostilities between them and bringing peace to Europe for fourteen months.

2. The origin of the phrase *to turn a blind eye* is often said to arise from an incident during the first Battle of Copenhagen, when the commander of the British fleet there signaled Nelson to withdraw if he felt it advisable. Lifting his glass to his blind eye, Nelson turned toward the signal flags, announced "I really do not see the signal," and fought on to victory.

3. After Trafalgar, the British Admiralty honored John Pollard, a midshipman on the HMS *Victory*, for avenging Lord Nelson's death. In *The Life of Nelson*, Robert Southey relates that Pollard and another midshipman, Francis Edward Collingwood, had returned fire at the French ship *Redoutable*. When only two snipers remained alive in her mizzen-top, Pollard shot one, then both Pollard and Collingwood shot the other after an old quartermaster, who'd recognized the Frenchman's distinctive hat and garb, identified him as the man who'd shot Nelson.

Southey mentions Guillemard in a footnote, for the matter of Nelson's death took a startling turn with the publication in Paris, in 1826, of the *Mémoires de Robert Guillemard, sergent en retraite, suivis de documens historiques, la plupart inédits, de 1805 à 1823*, a supposed autobiography of the French sniper who shot Nelson. The narrator recounted a life of such astonishing incident that the book aroused interest not only in France but in England and Germany as well, but it also met with skepticism because of many errors and grandiose, Zelig-like assertions. The author claimed, in particular, to have witnessed the assassination of Vice Admiral Pierre-Charles-Jean-Baptiste-Silvestre de Villeneuve, supposedly at the orders of Napoléon, in retaliation for his dismal performance in command of the French fleet at Trafalgar. Four years later, one J.A. Lardier confessed that he was the real author of the book and had invented Guillemard: "Lettre de l'auteur des Mémoires du sergent Robert Guillemard, publiés en 1826 et 1827, qui déclare que tout ce qu'il a raconté sur la mort du vice-amiral Villeneuve est une fiction, et que Guillemard est un personnage imaginaire," *Annales maritimes et coloniales*, 1830, 2ème partie, tome 2, pp. 185–87.

The Queen's Caprice

1. A little place called Le Pirli, village of Argentré, Laval district. (Author's note.)

2. *Septentrion* is an obsolete term meaning the "northern regions" or, simply, the "north."

Twenty Women in the Jardin du Luxembourg, Clockwise

1. For pictures of each statue and a brisk review of the lives of these remarkable women—and they are, all of them, even the mythical ones, remarkable women—consult the Internet to visit the site "ladies-of-luxembourg-garden.html." The statues are elegant and peaceful; the life stories behind many of them beggar description.

Civil Engineering

1. The brotherhood of the Fratres Pontifices was supposedly founded in the late twelfth century by Saint Bénézet, who, inspired by a vision, built the famous bridge over the Rhône at Avignon between 1177 and 1185. Saint Bénézet was a historical personage, but medieval scholars have essentially discounted as a romantic fiction the idea of a monastic order devoted to the pious work of helping pilgrims by building bridges, hospices, and ferry landings. Such work was almost always performed by lay organizations of masons and stonecutters hired on an ad hoc basis, but hagiographic works about Saint Bénézet popularized his legend and inspired early authors to elaborate upon these "brotherhoods," until historians of the late eighteenth century began correcting the record.

2. A voussoir is a wedge-shaped unit in an arch or vault. All such units are voussoirs, but the center piece at the apex or crown of the arch is the keystone. At the base of each side, or haunch, of the arch sits the lowest wedge-shaped unit, the springer. This piece "springs" up to begin the curve of the arch and itself rests on the impost, the top unit of the abutment supporting the haunch.

3. "Hej, Sloveni," naturally enough, means "Hey, Slavs!" and is an anthem dedicated to all Slavic peoples.

4. Nattier blue, a "moderate azure," is named after Jean-Marc Nattier, who became popular as a portrait painter at the court

of Louis XV, specializing in allegorical—and flattering—depictions of ladies in classical mythological attire.

Nitrox

1. Chimaeras, like sharks, are cartilaginous fish, but they branched off from those relatives about 400 million years ago, during which time they morphed into some very bizarre-looking creatures indeed. The "real" Chimera, after which they are named, was a fire-breathing monster composed of a lion, a goat, and a snake that was eventually killed by Bellerophon and the winged horse Pegasus. That immortal horse was sired by Poseidon out of the gorgon Medusa, from which comes the French word for jellyfish, *méduse*, so when Echenoz evokes *méduses*, *chimères*, *daphnies*, and so on, he is delicately skimming the abundance of mythological referents swimming around in the ocean.

Three Sandwiches at Le Bourget

1. This last story, a deceptively low-key affair, is full of dutifully noted street names mapping the narrator's peregrinations. France has been around for a long time and tends to avoid "Elm Street," etc., in favor of more robustly evocative names that often mean nothing to foreigners but offer instant backstory to the French. Such stories provide a valuable dimension to this text, so here is a bit of background for some of the more important street references, marked in the text by asterisks.

Notes

MAUBEUGE: Inhabited since about 256 A.D., this place has had a tumultuous history, passing in and out of various hands until landing in French ones for good in 1678. Maubeuge was besieged and taken by the Germans in 1914, who returned in 1940 to firebomb more than 90 percent of it—including the historic city center—into ashes.

DUNKIRK: Originally a fishing village on what is now the English Channel, Dunkirk was for centuries the plaything of Vikings, counts, kings, popes, dukes, archdukes, pirates, and various European nations. In May–June 1940 it was the scene of the Miracle of Dunkirk, in which more than 900 vessels evacuated some 340,000 Allied forces threatened by a German advance. During the German occupation, Allied bombers destroyed most of the town.

LA COURNEUVE: This small medieval village close to Paris eventually became a fashionable country retreat for the gentry, with two notable châteaus. In the 1960s, with immigration from former French colonies pressuring the expanding population of Paris, the construction of public and low-cost housing boomed in many suburbs of the capital, and the population of La Courneuve essentially doubled. Emblematic of La Courneuve's proud industrial past and turbulent history of working-class struggles, the Mécano factory, opened in 1914 and specializing in precision tool manufacturing, was finally forced to close in 1978 but will reopen as a multimedia and administrative center.

FRANCIS DE PRESSENSÉ (1853–1914): Born in Paris, Pressensé fought in the Franco-Prussian War (the War of 1870) and had distinguished careers in public service, the diplomatic corps, journalism, and politics. As a socialist he fought for the separation of church and state. During the Dreyfus affair (1894–1906), his support of Alfred Dreyfus and of Émile Zola's fiery campaign on his behalf cost Pressensé his membership in the National Order of the Legion of Honor, the highest French order of merit, the motto of which is *Honneur et Patrie* ("Honor and Country"). He does, however, now have the *honneur* of a few streets to his name in the *patrie*.

JEAN JAURÈS (1859–1914): Another defender of Alfred Dreyfus, Jaurès began as a moderate republican and wound up a socialist and antimilitarist and one of the most important writers and figures of the French Left. The founder of the (originally) socialist paper *L'Humanité*, he tried to help head off the Great War and was assassinated for his pains by a French nationalist at a Parisian café, now called Le Taverne du Croissant, marked by the traditional commemorative plaque.

DIVISION-LECLERC: It is impossible to overstate the affection and esteem in which Philippe François Marie Leclerc de Hauteclocque is held in France. Posthumously named a marshal of France, he is commonly known simply by his nom de guerre: Leclerc.

Born in 1902, this aristocratic soldier first fought the invading Germans in 1939, then went to French Equatorial Africa on the orders of General Charles de Gaulle in Britain. In 1943, Leclerc's force was reequipped by the Americans as the French Second Armored Division, the 2e DB, often called La Division Leclerc or Leclerc's Army. The 2e DB was shipped to Britain to participate in Operation Overlord, the Allied invasion of northern France, and landed at Utah Beach in Normandy in 1944 as part of General George S. Patton's U.S. Third Army. After liberating Paris, the 2e DB fought on the western front and in the final battles in southern Germany.

With the European war over in May 1945, Leclerc took command of the French Far East Expeditionary Corps and was France's representative at the surrender of the Japanese Empire on board the USS *Missouri* on September 2, 1945, in Tokyo Bay. Leclerc's mission was to regain control of French Indochina, but he soon realized that the situation demanded a diplomatic solution, and he warned the French and American politicians arrayed against Ho Chi Minh that nationalism, not communism, was the issue. He is said to have advised them to negotiate at any cost, in which case he was prescient indeed. He was replaced as commander of the French forces in 1946, and on November 28, 1947, he died with his staff in a plane crash in French Algeria.

DANIEL-CHARLES TRUDAINE (1703–69): This French administrator was a civil engineer of genius. One of the chief architects of the French road system, he is well known for the Trudaine Atlas, a monumental work (1745–80) of road maps and attendant features in astonishing cartographic and topographic detail: more than three thousand plates in sixty-two volumes, individually embellished with watercolor, showing actual and planned roads, waterways, the nature of the terrain, castles, houses, churches, cemeteries, ruins, plus designs for bridges, canals, and other civil engineering projects. Look up "Atlas de Trudaine—Wikipédia" to see a few of these lovely plates, the satellite photos of their day, and "L'atlas de

Trudaine—YouTube" will bring you a French video about the book.

8 MAI: At three o'clock on May 8, 1945, Victory in Europe Day, church bells rang throughout France to mark Nazi Germany's unconditional surrender to the Allies of World War II. General Charles de Gaulle paid his respects at the Tomb of the Unknown Soldier under the Arc de Triomphe, and all around the world there was, naturally, dancing in the streets.

2. Erik Satie (1866–1925) was a French composer, pianist, writer, and eccentric whose unconventional compositions were much admired by his contemporaries in the Parisian avant-garde, including Mallarmé, Verlaine, Breton, Man Ray, Cocteau, and Picasso. Debussy, Milhaud, Poulenc, Ravel, and Stravinsky were among those influenced by his ideas, which presaged such later artistic movements as musique concrète, indeterminacy, and minimalism. The youthful anarchist Satie became a socialist and in 1914, after the assassination of Jean Jaurès, joined the French Section of the Workers' International. He never invited anyone home to his bleak studio without water or electricity in the southern suburbs of Paris, where after his death his friends found scores of umbrellas, several identical backup suits of gray velvet (his customary attire), and two tied-together, out-of-tune pianos full of unopened letters.

3. A French singer-songwriter and poet, Jean Ferrat (1930–2010) was known for singing poems, particularly the work of Louis Aragon. When his Russian-born father was deported

to Auschwitz in 1942, Ferrat left school to go to work. He released his second single, "Ma Môme," in 1960. Googling "Paroles Ma môme de Jean Ferrat, Clip Ma môme" will bring up a video of the song and provide the text of the French lyrics, the gist of which is "My girl's not stuck-up, doesn't act like a movie star, doesn't wear dark glasses, and she works in a factory in Créteil"—a town in the southeastern suburbs of Paris.

4. Ordering French sandwiches separates the wheat from the chaff. Requesting *un sandwich au jambon* will get you a ham sandwich—made of bread and ham. If you want that sandwich with butter, you order *un jambon beurre*, a "ham butter." A ham-and-cheese sandwich is not a "ham sandwich with cheese" *(un sandwich au jambon avec du fromage)*, but a "ham cheese" *(un jambon fromage)*. Which does not include butter! *Un saucisson sec* means a salami, a "dry sausage," and if it's a sandwich order, it means salami and bread, period. No butter. To get *that*, you order *un sec-beurre*: a "dry butter." Go figure.

5. Elected by universal male suffrage to draw up a constitution after the overthrow of the monarchy, the Convention Nationale governed France from September 20, 1792, until October 26, 1795, a crucial time for the French Revolution. The Convention's internal power struggles are the stuff of legend, and the most famous of its avatars is the Committee of Public Safety, a triumph of Orwellian doublespeak. Created to defend the fledgling republic against internal rebellion and foreign attack, this committee essentially ruled France during the Reign of Terror (1793–94). As internal repression accelerated,

an antireligious campaign to dechristianize society—through execution if necessary—culminated in a celebration of Reason in Notre Dame on November 10, 1793. The intransigent Maximilien de Robespierre, however, denounced this cult and sent many of its practitioners to the guillotine. In June 1794 he announced his own establishment of a new state religion, the deistic Cult of the Supreme Being. This cult, too, was short-lived, however, for it died with its creator on July 28, 1794, when Robespierre, who had sent so many of his former allies to the guillotine, followed them to the scaffold.

6. In 1815 the Bourbon monarchy was restored in France, but when Napoléon escaped from the island of Elba on February 26 and returned to rule in Paris, Louis XVIII fled the country. The French defeat at Waterloo on June 18 led to Napoléon's abdication and exile on Saint Helena, the return of Louis XVIII, and the Second Treaty of Paris, which finally ended the Napoleonic Wars (1792–1815) and made peace between France and her adversaries Great Britain, Prussia, Austria, and Russia.

7. Chancellor Otto von Bismarck goaded the French into declaring war on Prussia on July 19, 1870, thus drawing the other German states to his side in the Franco-Prussian War. Soundly beaten, France not only lost most of Alsace and some parts of Lorraine but witnessed the unification of Germany under Wilhelm I of Prussia, crowned kaiser of this new and threateningly powerful German state in the Hall of Mirrors at Versailles on January 18, 1871. Fueled by anger over France's humiliation and the monarchist sympathies of the Assemblée

Nationale, a revolutionary uprising broke out two months later in Montmartre, but the socialist government of the Paris Commune held power in the capital for only two months and was crushed by the French army in a week of carnage during La Semaine Sanglante (May 21–28).

8. Google *"gueules cassées"* and click under "Images"; the injuries are stunning.

Jean Echenoz won France's prestigious Prix Goncourt for *I'm Gone* (The New Press). He is the author of eleven novels in English translation—including *1914*, *Big Blondes*, *Lightning*, *Piano*, *Ravel*, and *Running*, all published by The New Press—and the winner of numerous literary prizes, among them the Prix Médicis and the European Literature Jeopardy Prize. He lives in Paris.

Linda Coverdale's most recent translation for The New Press was Jean Echenoz's *1914*. She was the recipient of the French-American Foundation's 2008 Translation Prize for her translation of Echenoz's *Ravel* (The New Press). She lives in Brooklyn.

PUBLISHING IN THE PUBLIC INTEREST

Thank you for reading this book published by The New Press. The New Press is a nonprofit, public interest publisher. New Press books and authors play a crucial role in sparking conversations about the key political and social issues of our day.

We hope you enjoyed this book and that you will stay in touch with The New Press. Here are a few ways to stay up to date with our books, events, and the issues we cover:

- Sign up at www.thenewpress.com/subscribe to receive updates on New Press authors and issues and to be notified about local events
- Like us on Facebook: www.facebook.com/newpress books
- Follow us on Twitter: www.twitter.com/thenewpress

Please consider buying New Press books for yourself; for friends and family; or to donate to schools, libraries, community centers, prison libraries, and other organizations involved with the issues our authors write about.

The New Press is a 501(c)(3) nonprofit organization. You can also support our work with a tax-deductible gift by visiting www.thenewpress.com/donate.